A FEATI

Dic
Illustrator: Wendy Theobald

CHILD'S PLAY—NUT'S AWAY!
Gerald Hampshire
Illustrator: John Claypole

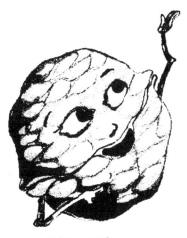

Willie Walnut

Author royalties and illustrator fees
donated to:
The Cancer Research Campaign

WWB CHILDREN'S
NORWICH, NR8 6YN

© "A Feathered Magi" Richard Bradshaw (story), 00
© "Child's Play—Nuts Away!" Gerald Hampshire (story), 00
© October 00, this edition Wendy Webb
© Illustrations for "A Feathered Magi" Wendy Theobald, 00
© Illustrations for "Child's Play—Nuts Away!" John
Claypole, 00
© Puzzles, Wendy Webb, 00

ISBN: 1-903264-19-7
British Library Cataloguing-in-Publication Data
A catalogue record for this book is available from the British Library.

Published by: Wendy Webb Books
Distribution: Wendy Webb
PO Box 210, Taverham NORWICH, NR8 6WX

With grateful thanks to our illustrators Wendy Theobald and John Claypole who have waived their fees for this charity publication. You may also help by purchasing posters (see Activity Pages).

WWB CHILDREN'S
Reading guide: 5-8 year olds

To Eleanor
with best wishes
from Dick Shaw.

As they flew towards the rocky crag

A FEATHERED MAGI
Dick Shaw

The three birds felt totally exhausted as they flew towards the rocky crag where Lord Eagle lived.

"I suppose we'd better stop off and pay our respects," said the weary robin. "There's bound to be trouble if we don't," retorted the jackdaw.

The starling gripped a small flat piece of wood in his beak, so he couldn't say anything.

Lord Eagle
was renowned
for his size and
power

Lord Eagle was renowned for his
size and power, but not for
having a sunny disposition.
"What do you want?" he
enquired gruffly, as the three
weary birds landed beside his
huge and untidy nest.

The robin, smallest and bravest
of the three, replied on their
behalf. "We had a vision from

4

BINGKRID, telling us that a very special nestling is about to hatch in the Wild Forest. We are going to pay our respects. Perhaps you would like to come with us, Mighty One?"

"No, I wouldn't, you foolish little creature. Other birds pay their respects to me, as you have wisely chosen to do. Not the other way round."

Lord Eagle flapped his great wings to emphasize the point and the poor starling was so scared that he nearly snapped his precious piece of wood.

"Tell me, why should BINGKRID, God of all Flying Creatures, honour you three with such a vision as you choose

Lord Eagle flapped his great wings
(page 5)

to claim? I am the all-powerful one and I have received no such vision of a special nestling being born."

"We really don't know ourselves why we have been so honoured. We don't even know what kind of bird it is," confessed the jackdaw.

"It is bound to be a majestic bird of prey, like me. Now listen, if you should happen to find this special creature of your vision, call back here and let me know. I may decide on a personal visit after all. Until such time, be off with you and take your silly stories, and yourselves, elsewhere!"

The great ferocious eagle turned his back on them in dismissal,

The great star is hovering directly above that
massive old tree (page 9)

so the three birds took off and flew onwards. By day a sort of sixth sense guided them, but by night a beautiful diamond-like star twinkled ahead of them as they flew.

After several days and nights of travel, "This is it!" exclaimed the jackdaw. "I just know it is. Look, my friends, the great star is hovering directly above that massive old tree".
The three travelling companions swooped down towards a huge oak tree in the very heart of the Wild Forest.
They found a nest with lots of chirpy sparrows bobbing along to it, presenting bits of moss to the gentle thrush sitting there.

Lots of chirpy sparrows bobbing along (page 9)

Further along one of the twin boughs supporting the nest, a male thrush hovered anxiously. He looked almost shy, as part of this serene picture.

Humbly the three birds approached the female thrush and the robin, in great pain, pulled one of the finest red feathers from his breast and gave it to her. Meanwhile the jackdaw was poking about amongst the feathers beneath his wing, at the point where it joined his body. He produced a gleaming silver ring he had stolen from one of those awful human creatures. They were even more dangerous than mighty Lord Eagle.

The robin pulled one of the finest red feathers from his breast (page 10)

Presenting his ring to the serene-looking thrush and her nestling made all the risk seem well worthwhile.

The tiny bird peeping out from beneath his mother's
feathers (page 13)

Finally the starling gratefully dropped his burden into the nest, careful not to hit the tiny bird peeping out from beneath his mother's feathers. On a piece of wood was a pleasing picture that the starling had carved with his sharp pointed beak. It was not easy and it had taken him a long time. But he could tell that the gentle bird liked his offering, for she sang again especially for him.

While these unusual gifts were given, the drab little sparrows had backed off, as if feeling unworthy to mix their humble offerings with the more exciting gifts from these three weary travellers from afar.

He flew up to warn the travellers
(page 16)

"Bless their little hearts", said
the gentle thrush. "They mean
well and they have so little to
offer when it comes to plumage

or song. But my little one is really snug and warm, thanks to the moss they have brought me for lining my nest".

The jackdaw was about to point out that, in his opinion, sparrows were little more than thieving urchins of the trees and hedgerows. Suddenly he remembered how he had come by his gift of a precious silver ring. He thought it best, under the circumstances, to keep his thoughts and comments to himself. So the happy mood of the meeting was not broken.

Their duty, according to the vision from BINGKRID, was now completed. The three birds thought it best that they should be on their way.

Lower down on the tree, in the hollow part of the trunk, lived a wise old owl. He flew up to warn the travellers. On his advice, three exhausted but happy birds did not return to Lord Eagle to explain the exact whereabouts of the nest.

As for what happened to the very special nestling they had seen so briefly, peeping out from beneath his mother's feathers. Well, that's another story.

THE END

Peeping out from beneath his mother's feathers

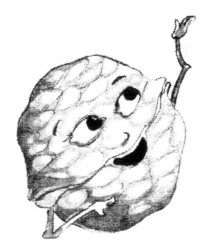

Willie Walnut

CHILD'S PLAY—NUT'S AWAY!

Gerald Hampshire

Willie Walnut jumped out of the fruit bowl and landed on a little patch of moonlight on the kitchen floor.

"Goodbye friends," he shouted cheerfully.

"Wherever are you going?" asked Charlie Chestnut.

"I'm going to be a tree!" replied Willie proudly.

"Ooooh!" cried all the nuts.

"I'm going to meet Alfie Acorn in the garden," he told them. "He knows what to do."

"It's cold outside," said Audrey Almond.

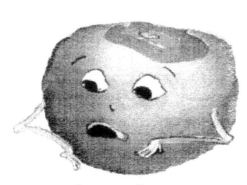

Charlie Chestnut

"And it rains," Charlie Chestnut added. Hilary Hazelnut peeped over the side of the fruit bowl. "Can I be a tree, Willie?" she enquired, sweetly.

"No you can't!" boomed Charlie Chestnut.

"You're staying here with us."
Willie jumped back inside the fruit bowl and

Hilary Hazelnut

stared hard at Charlie Chestnut. "She can come with me if she wants," he told him sharply. "It's nothing to do with you."

"But it's cold outside," Audrey Almond wailed again.

Willie jumped on to the edge of the fruit bowl and looked down at them all. "Listen," he said firmly. "One day the nutcracker will come for you."

"Oh no!" they all cried, and the fruit bowl rocked from side to side as the nuts shivered in fear. Charlie Chestnut was shocked. "Can I be a tree, Willie?" he pleaded. Willie looked doubtful. "Well..."
"We all want to be trees!" cried the nuts.

Willie Walnut

All right then," Willie said at last. "But you will have to do as Alfie Acorn tells you."
"We will! We will!" chorused the nuts.
"I'll fetch him then," said Willie.

When he returned a little later, a surprised murmur spread through the nuts. Alfie Acorn had a crown on his head. He looked just like a king.

"Gather round," he said importantly.
The nuts crowded round him eagerly.
"Anyone who wants to be a tree will have to go to Green

Alfie Acorn

Town," he told them.
"Where's Green Town?" asked the nuts.
"Why, I thought everyone knew where Green Town was!" he replied, surprised. "It's over the fields, near the school. The children have built a nature reserve. They have planted wild flowers, bushes, <u>trees</u>." He paused for it to sink in.

"All the wild animals and insects visit it, and the children guard it carefully."

"Will there be any nutcrackers?" asked Audrey Almond.

Alfie chuckled. "I don't think so."

"No more questions," said Willie firmly. "We've got a long way to go."

They all went into the garden. Then, like a long winding snake, they followed Alfie Acorn across the fields to Green Town.

It was still dark when they arrived, and they were very, very tired.

"I'm fed up," Charlie Chestnut grumbled.

"And it's too cold for me," Audrey Almond moaned.

Charlie Chestnut

"Listen everybody!" shouted Alfie.

"All we have to do now is go into the greenhouse and wait for the children. When they see us they will find us a home in a nice seed tray. Then we will start to grow into trees."

"It's too cold," Audrey Almond moaned again.

Alfie sniffed.

Audrey Almond

"You can go to the tropical house." He touched his crown and announced, proudly, "I'm not afraid of the cold. I'm going to be an oak tree!"

Willie Walnut looked at Hilary Hazelnut "Would you like to come with me?" he asked.

Hilary blushed. "I'd love to," she replied shyly.

They went into the greenhouse together, and snuggled up inside a big, green seed tray.

When the children arrived they planted all the nuts. They nursed them carefully, and in a while they started to grow.

When they grew into baby trees, the children planted them outside in the fresh air.

Audrey Almond decided to stay in the tropical house. It was very warm in there, but she still managed to complain now and then!

Alfie Acorn would grow into a big, sturdy oak tree someday.

Then he would have lots of little acorns, all with little crowns on their heads! Hilary Hazelnut and Willie

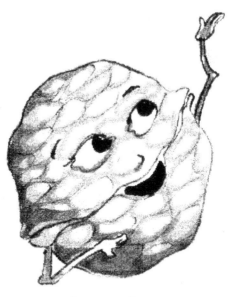

Willie Walnut

Walnut grew close together and sometimes, when the wind blew, their branches touched one another.

One day the trees would reward the children for their kindness. They would fill Green Town with the scent of their blossoms.

THE END

ACTIVITY PAGES—A FEATHERED MAGI

Try and match up the birds to the people from the Bible story of the Three Wise Men. Ask someone to help you find and read the story in the New Testament, near the end of the Bible:-
Eagle (Matthew chapter 2 verses 1-2)
Sparrows (Luke chapter 2 verses 8 and 16)
Mummy Thrush (Matthew chapter 2 verse 11)
Daddy Thrush (Matthew chapter 1 verse 20)
Baby Thrush (Matthew chapter 2 verse 1)
Robin, Jackdaw and **Starling** (Matthew chapter 2 verse 11)
Owl (Matthew chapter 2 verses 12-13)
Bingkrid (Luke chapter 1 verse 26)

"Bingkrid" is a mixed up word. Can you unjumble the letters to find out what sort of bird Bingkrid is?

Now design a Christmas card, using the birds from "A Feathered Magi". Make up a Christmas greeting for inside your card, using the words of one bird from the story.

Send a copy of your card to Wendy Webb Books, and you will receive 10% off your next order for children's books:
Wendy Webb (FM/CARD), PO Box 210, Taverham, Norwich, NR8 6WX.

ACTIVITY PAGES–CHILD'S PLAY–NUTS AWAY!

Unscramble all the words below, from the story:
Clarieh Chuntste
Fiela Croan
Lilwie Lawtun
Rhialy Lazethun
Drauey Monald.
You may buy two posters from Child's Play—Nuts Away! One A4 laminated poster costs £2.00 or you can buy both for £3.00 post free.*
A) All trees from the story, brief description, details of leaves and fruit.
B) All the cartoon nuts from the story.
Also colouring sheets of B) 20p each (minimum order £2.00 post free). ***20% to charity.**

NOW ask your family to take you out around your nearest park, woodland or waste ground. See how many trees you can identify from their leaves and their nuts.
Ask your family about the trees not pictured. You may also like to ask your teacher, or visit your local library for pictures of more trees and their fruit.
Write a letter to your local council and ask if they are planting any trees in your area—they may have a tree-planting and they need children and schools to help them.
ANSWERS: Copy free from Wendy Webb Books.

WENDY WEBB BOOKS
ORDER FORM

NAME:_____

ADDRESS:_____

_____

Please write quantity required:

ADVENTURE SERIES Jim Beeton, £6.50

☐ inclusive (all 3 titles)

GRABBIT & SKOOT SERIES Alan

☐ Cliff £6.50 (2 books, 1 cuddly squirrel)

JACK THE STATION CAT GOES TO

☐ SCHOOL SERIES (1) Alan Cliff £2.95

DAVID SERIES Wendy Webb £16.50

☐ (all 7 books) OR £20 (incl. "Beautiful Child") OR £10 (4 books); PERS avail.

A FEATHERED MAGI (1) Dick Shaw

☐ with CHILD'S PLAY, £2.95.

A FEATHERED FOLLOWING (2) Dick

☐ Shaw, £TBA, reserve your copy today

A FEATHERED MINISTRY (3) Dick

☐ Shaw, £TBA, reserve your copy today

A FEATHERED FAREWELL (4) Dick

☐ Shaw, £TBA, reserve your copy today

THE LAST FOX Gerald Hampshire,

☐ £2.95, Jan 01, reserve today

ORDERS: Wendy Webb (FM), PO Box 210, Taverham, Norwich, NR8 6WX.

PHONE: 0798-917 4076.

☐ BUY <u>ANY 5 FOR £10.00</u> post free (any children's books in print @ Oct 00).